TOP THAT! Kids™

Copyright © 2003 Top That! Publishing plc,
Tide Mill Way, Woodbridge, Suffolk, IP12 1AP, UK
Top That! is a Registered Trademark of Top That! Publishing plc
All rights reserved
www.topthatpublishing.com

Shooting Stars

Written by Jennifer Anne Cromar
Illustrated by Angela Terris

When it is dark,
And the sun is away.

Sparkle wakes up.
It's the start of her day!

She is off to meet Jessie,
Whizzing in the sky

Collecting lots of twinkling stars
As she flutters by.

Pretty lights for the party
Will make it oh so bright.

She must collect lots and lots,
The party's tomorrow night!

Finished looking for treasure
And back down on the ground.

Excited to show Jessie
All the stars she has found!

"Good evening, Jessie.
Have you had a nice day?

It is so great to see you.
Let's go out to play!"

Together fairies flutter
Into a darker night.

They say hello to all the bats
That give them both a fright!

They fly around the universe
travelling so very far.

Through the astral heavens
To find the perfect star.

Swooping and swirling,
And having such fun.

But then crash! Where's Jessie?
Oh no! What's she done?

Poor Jessie, She's so clumsy.
"Are you feeling okay?"

"It's not easy flying at night.
It's simple in the day!"

"I'm getting too sleepy"
says Jessie with a moan.

"I think that it's time that
we should head for home."

On the way down to the ground,
Sparkle sees something glow.

"What's that down there?" asks Jessie.
"Oh, I think I know..."

It is their friends, the glow worms
come out to say hello.

They thank Jessie for the invites.
Of course they'd love to go!

Jess and Sparkle join them
And chat for a minute or two.

They say goodbye, must get busy.
There's still so much to do.

The bigger stars will be stepping stones
to make a well-lit lawn.

Now Jessie must go off to bed,
So tired, she starts to yawn.

Whilst the moonlight beams and gleams
With much more work to do,

Sparkle sprinkles fairy dust
To help make dreams come true.

Now Sparkle's back up in the sky
To catch some bright moon beams.

Night fairies are so busy,
Whilst we are in our dreams.

Be careful, Sparkle! Look behind you.
There's a shooting star so fast.

Nimbly she darts out of the way,
And watches the star flash past.

Sparkle's bag is full and heavy.
The sun begins to rise.

Time to go back to Jessie's and
Leave a celestial surprise.

She flies back down to Jessie's house,
leaves her star bag by the door.

Jessie, of course, is sound asleep.
Can you hear her snore?

Walking back down the path
Sparkle sees Mr. Snail.

He is lazily going home,
leaving a shiny trail.

Even though Sparkle is starting to fade,
They talk for a little while.

"Better go home now, Mr. Snail"
And she leaves him with a smile.

"Bye bye Sparkle," says Mr. Snail,
"See you on party night".

She flutters home, straight to bed,
Just as the dawn gets bright.